No More Yawning!

D0191966

ALIS

2639531

For my sister Coral – Paeony Lewis
Welcome to the world Charlie! – Brita Granström

© 2008 The Chicken House
First published in the United Kingdom in 2008 by
The Chicken House, 2 Palmer Street, Frome, Somerset, BA11 1DS
www.doublecluck.com

Text © 2008 Paeony Lewis
Illustrations © 2008 Brita Granström

All rights reserved
No part of this publication may be reproduced or transmitted or utilized in any
form or by any means, electronic, mechanical, photocopying or otherwise, without
the prior permission of the publisher

The moral rights of the author and illustrator have been asserted

Designed by Ian Butterworth

Printed and bound in Singapore by Imago

British Library Cataloguing in Publication Data available
Library of Congress Cataloguing in Publication data available

HB ISBN: 978-1-905294-31-2
PB ISBN: 978-1-905294-68-8

No More Yawning!

Paeony Lewis Illustrated by Brita Granström

Chicken House

I'm **Florence.**
This is my drawing of **Arnold** in a **banana bed.**
I'm getting him into a **sleepy** mood
because it's **seven o'clock** and
time for **bed.**

ABERDEENSHIRE LIBRARY AND	
INFORMATION SERVICES	
2639531	
HJ	719911
JP	£5.99
JU	SURB

Mum kisses me goodnight and dims my light. I yawn a **big, BIG** yawn and shut my eyes.

I yawn again. This time my yawn's so BIG, it's bigger than a banana.

banana

sad

monkey

We're trying to **sleep**, we **really** are, but we can't. The trouble is, Mum forgot to give Arnold a goodnight kiss.

We find Mum. Mum kisses Arnold. I kiss Mum.
Arnold wants another kiss.
'No more kissing.
No more yawning,' says Mum.
'It's time for sleep.'

We're **trying** to **sleep,** we really are.
But Arnold's feeling lonely so I sing him a lullaby
about a twinkling star. Arnold
likes it so much I have to
sing it five times.

twinkle

Then I have to draw him a picture of a

shiny
bright
star.

All the singing makes me thirsty. So I go to find Mum. Mum gives me a cup of water and I only spill a bit when I **yawn** a **yawn** bigger than Arnold's smile.

Mum says, 'No more **singing.**
No more **yawning.**
It's time for **sleep.**'

smile

yawn

We're trying to sleep, we really are.
But Arnold wants a story. He says it has to be
about a monkey and a giant banana tree.
  I hunt through all my books, but I can't
find that story. So I make it up. Though telling
a story isn't easy
when you can't
stop yawning.

giant **BIG** tree ↑

happy monkey

Arnold wants pictures too.
So I start drawing.

Oops, Mum's seen my bedroom light. I jump into bed and yawn a yawn bigger than Arnold's tummy.

Mum frowns at all the books
and says,
      'No more stories.
No more yawning.
It's time for sleep.'
      But we're trying to sleep,
we really are.
      Mum tells me I'll get sleepy
if I count imaginary sheep
jumping over a gate.

yawn

Arnold

tummy

sheep

So I try counting sheep.
One, two, three, four. Six? Five?
I've gone wrong. Sometimes I play with cut-out
numbers so tonight I make cut-out sheep. I number
them. One, two, three, four, five, six, seven . . .

What's after seven? Arnold thinks it's **nine**. It's hard to count sheep when you can't stop yawning.

Nine, ten, eleven, twelve . . . What's after twelve? I don't know.

Arnold doesn't know. We have to ask Mum.

I yawn a yawn bigger than Arnold's tail to show Mum that we're trying to sleep, we really are. It's not our fault numbers are so tricky.

Mum groans and says,
'No more counting, no more drawing, no more cutting, no more yawning.
It's time for sleep.'

She tells me I'll get sleepy if I shut my eyes and think of everything that's yellow. And if I'm still not asleep I can choose another colour. Then another.

I shut my eyes tight.
Sun. Butter. My yellow chair.
Grandpa's hat. Sunflowers.
Buttercups. Cheese. Our car.
What else is yellow? Bananas!

We're trying to **sleep**, we **really** are. But I can't think of anything else that's yellow. Arnold can't either. So we think about **pink**.

My **curtains** are very pink.
And **candyfloss**. Raspberry milkshake.
Pink socks. What else? Are my big **yawns** pink?
We're not sure. I call out to ask Mum.

Mum's cross. She says:
'No more kissing.
No more singing.
No more stories.
No more counting.
No more drawing.
No more cutting.
No more colours.

We're trying to sleep, we really are. But it's hard to sleep when you're sad.

Mum says sorry for shouting and gives me a hug. And Arnold too.

I ask Mum how she got to sleep when she was little.

Mum thinks hard. Then she remembers. She'd shut her eyes and make up a story in her head. Soon she'd be dreaming about fairies or digging up treasure.

I tell Mum my dream story will be
about exploring a jungle full of monkeys,
bananas, wild animals . . .
I yawn a yawn **bigger** than Arnold
and shut my eyes. . .

monkeys

bananas

wild animals

We were asleep, we really were.
Totally, completely asleep. Then Mum woke us
with a noisy yawn as big as an elephant!
Naughty Mum!

elephant

noisy
yawn

I tell Mum, 'No more yawning.
It's time YOU went to sleep!'

And I give
her a kiss.
'Goodnight!'

Tips on Getting to Sleep

Mum thinks I'm a NUISANCE at bedtime. I think that having to sleep for twelve hours is the NUISANCE. Unfortunately, I'm told I HAVE to sleep because that's when my body grows and my brain sorts itself out and my mum rests. So here are some more tips from me and Mum on getting to sleep.

●●●●●●●●●●●●●●●●●●●●●●●●●●●●●

No Naps

When I was very little I needed a nap in the afternoon. Now it stops me sleeping at night if I fall asleep in the day. Though it's hard to stop my eyes closing when Mum starts chatting to a friend when we're out shopping.

Bla, bla, bla, bla

Lots of Exercise

It's really hard to sleep when my body feels all fidgety and isn't tired. Mum says that happens when I haven't done much exercise like swimming, cycling or throwing Arnold into trees in the park. Monkeys like swinging in trees, though sometimes Arnold leaps too high and once he stayed out all night until the wind blew him down, so I couldn't sleep because I was so worried.

Soft Music

Sometimes it's noisy at night where I live. So I listen to a CD of soft music to help drown out voices and stuff. Arnold likes a CD that sounds like a storm in a banana rainforest.

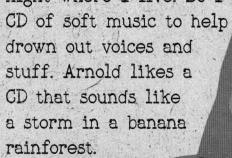

Regular Bedtime
Mum gets cross with Dad when he lets me stay up really late. She says I must always go to bed and wake up at the same time so my body learns when it's time to sleep. I tell Mum that my body doesn't have a good memory.

Relaxing Routine
Mum insists on a relaxing bedtime routine. That means no showers (they wake me up) or too much splashing and bouncing in the bath. But sitting quietly in a warm bath with lavender bubbles is boring! After my bath, it's story-time. I like lots of stories, but Mum yawns after about six. Then it's bed and a kiss goodnight for Arnold and me.

No Cola
Mum says cola contains caffeine and will keep me awake and bouncy. So I have warm milk and a plain biscuit to relax me – yawn.

Darkness
I have thick curtains to keep out the light in summer. Though if it's too dark then Arnold worries there's a gorilla hiding in the wardrobe. So we have a dim night-light in case he wakes up at night. Arnold says it's like the moon shining in the jungle.

Grrrr...

Sweeeet Dreams!

Do you remember your **dreams?** As soon as I wake up I think about my dreams. Then I grab paper and crayons and draw what I can remember (sometimes it's hard to remember). Here are some pictures I've stuck in my **Dream Scrapbook.** You could try it too.

Florence
Scrap-
BOOK

Dreams